Barney
The Boat Dog

Very Brave Dog

For Alan and Arran, in memory of a very hot day
at Stoke Bruerne

This edition first published in 2011 by Usborne Publishing Ltd., Usborne House,
83-85 Saffron Hill, London EC1N 8RT, England.
www.usborne.com

Copyright © Linda Newbery, 2011
First published as Whistling Jack © Linda Newbery, 1997
Illustrations © Usborne Publishing Ltd., 2011

The right of Linda Newbery to be identified as the author
of this work has been asserted by her in accordance with the Copyright,
Designs and Patents Act, 1988.

Cover illustration by John Butler, johnbutlerart.com
Illustrations by John Francis, courtesy of Bernard Thornton Artists, London

The name Usborne and the devices 🔱 🌐 are Trade Marks of
Usborne Publishing Ltd.

This is a work of fiction. The characters, incidents, and dialogues are products
of the author's imagination and are not to be construed as real. Any resemblance
to actual events or persons, living or dead, is entirely coincidental.

A CIP catalogue record for this book is available from the British Library.

JFMAMJJA OND/16 04415/01 ISBN 9781409521983
Printed in India.

Barney
The Boat Dog

Very Brave Dog

Linda Newbery

Illustrated by John Francis

USBORNE

Chapter One

Barney was a narrowboat dog. That doesn't
mean that he was particularly narrow – in
fact he was a little on the plump side. But
Whistling Jack, the boat he lived on, *was*
narrow. *Whistling Jack* was a long, low boat,
thin enough to fit through the tightest lock
gates and the narrowest stretches of canal.

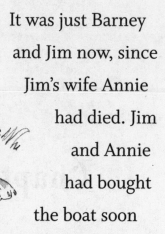

It was just Barney and Jim now, since Jim's wife Annie had died. Jim and Annie had bought the boat soon after their grown-up son left home and got married. First they moved to a smaller house, one with a canal running past the gardens. From there they could watch the narrowboats going past, and soon they thought of having a boat of their own. Jim had always wanted a boat, and Annie liked the idea too.

They named their boat *Whistling Jack*. Whistling Jack was the name of a wild plant they'd seen on an island holiday –

tall-stemmed, with pinky-purple flowers. They both thought the new name was just right, and *Whistling Jack* seemed to like it, too. Soon the boat was freshly-painted in bright new colours, and Annie painted pinky-purple Whistling Jacks on the door panels where other boats had roses and castles.

They kept *Whistling Jack* moored at the end of their garden, and every summer they used to set off in the boat for a few weeks: the three of them, Annie, Jim and Barney.

But then Annie died. Jim missed her so much that he couldn't bear to live in the house any more. Barney missed Annie too, but he tried to be as lively and bouncy as he could, for Jim's sake.

After several gloomy months, Jim sold
the house with all its happy and sad
memories, and now *Whistling Jack* was
home for himself and Barney.

Although it would have been better
still if Annie had been with them, Barney
loved his new life on the canals and rivers.

Whistling Jack was a moving home. One week they might be in London on the Thames, chugging slowly past Big Ben; the next week they might be out in the country, moored to a quiet riverbank with only ducks for company.

To show that he was a boat dog, Barney wore a collar with a disc engraved *Barney* on one side and *Whistling Jack* on the other, with a little picture of a narrowboat. As they approached a lock, he would stand at the prow of *Whistling Jack* and bark when he saw the lock gates coming into view.

Inside *Whistling Jack*, Jim and Barney had everything they wanted. The boat was not quite two metres wide, so everything had to fit neatly into its place. There was a tiny kitchen (galley, it was properly called) with a cooker, a fridge and cupboards. Behind that was a sitting room and a table. Next came a mini-bathroom with a toilet and shower, and finally the bedroom, which had two bunks: the lower one for Jim, the top one for Barney. Barney slept curled up on a blanket, and his bunk was at just the right height for him to look out of the porthole window and see what was happening outside.

Everything Jim owned had to fit into the cupboards or in the spaces underneath the bunk and sofa. He even had a garden – flower pots in painted canalware on the roof and decks, filled with geraniums, petunias and ivy.

Annie had loved her plants, and now Jim looked after them, watering them each morning, and evenings as well when the weather was really hot.

Every few days Jim and Barney needed to stop for water or fuel, or to buy food at one of the canalside stores. On warm evenings in summer, when Jim had moored up, they could sit out on the deck

while Jim did his crossword or read a book,
and Barney looked at the other boats
going by.

On cold winter nights Jim closed the
doors snugly, drew the curtains and turned
on the radio, and brewed cocoa on his
little stove.

Barney liked summer best, when he could lie on the roof and daydream, and when people walked along the towpath and admired *Whistling Jack*'s bright paintwork and the pots of flowers. Sometimes they exclaimed to each other: "*Whistling Jack*! That's a funny name!" or "Oh, look at the little dog on the roof!"

Barney liked attention. He knew that people thought he was clever, especially when he raced from one lock gate to the other, waiting for the water to rush through. "You'd think he understood how it works!" people said.

Huh! Of course Barney understood. He'd seen it happening enough times. He knew more about it than most people did. He still found it exciting, though, when Jim opened the sluices with his special handle, freeing a torrent of water.

Whistling Jack, waiting in the space between the two gates, would be lifted up by the water if they were travelling upstream, or lowered gently to the next level if they were travelling down. Barney liked to leap ashore as they pulled in to the lock, and he always knew exactly when to jump on board again, when the water reached the right level and Jim was ready to open the gates at the other end.

Often, they met people in hired holiday boats who got into all sorts of trouble at the locks. They'd lose their handles, or forget to tie up their boat when they got off, or have all the sluices open at once and then wonder why the water level wasn't right.

Barney didn't know how people could

get themselves into such a muddle. It was
simple, really, when you'd seen it done as
many times as Barney had.

Chapter Two

Hayford Lock was one of Jim's favourite places on the canal, because he liked going through the tunnel.

Jim and Barney were on their way from London to Yorkshire to visit Jim's brother. As Hayford Lock was a good place to stop for water and shopping, Barney wasn't surprised when Jim moored up there. It was a busy place, especially on a hot summer Saturday like today. There were cafés and ice-cream stalls and a museum, and people could take boat-rides up and down the canal.

Barney only liked stopping at Hayford Lock if they were travelling the other way, back to London. That would mean the tunnel was safely behind them. Going *this* way, he worried and fretted. He couldn't stop thinking about what faced him a short distance farther on. It was the longest, darkest tunnel he had seen, lasting for over 800 metres. In his imagination, it had no end at all. He thought of the entrance gaping like a huge mouth and throat, waiting to swallow him up.

Barney had been through the tunnel four times before, but he didn't think he'd ever stop being frightened, or understand why Jim liked it. Barney hated the dripping water and the echoey sound, and the smoky smell from the engines of the boats that went through. So much water dripped from the roof that Jim had to put on his raincoat, even when it was perfectly dry outside. And it was so dark that Jim had to turn on *Whistling Jack*'s headlamp.

Even in summer, it was a cold, frightening place. Barney still trembled when he remembered the first time they'd gone through, even though it was more than two years ago. He had pressed himself against Jim's legs as the tunnel swallowed them up. Barney barked, and another dog

seemed to bark back at him – a fierce, echoey dog, from somewhere in the blackness. Barney didn't dare bark again. He tried not to let the dark press against his ears too hard and he kept his gaze firmly fixed on the glimmer of light at the far end, which slowly grew into a space big enough for the boat to slide through.

He was so terrified that he had nightmares about it for the next three nights.

After that, every time they went through tunnels, even short ones, Barney would slink down the steps, go to his bunk and curl up on his blanket, and wait for Jim to whistle to him when they were out in the open. Then he'd rush all the way from one end of *Whistling Jack* to the other, three times, and even (if it was a warm day) have a celebratory swim in the canal. Jim liked to see Barney swimming and would throw a ball for him to fetch, but he didn't like it so much when Barney shook himself dry, showering cold water everywhere.

Today was a *very* warm day. There were lots of people walking along the canalside, looking at the boats, taking photographs and waiting for rides. Barney tried to enjoy the holiday mood, and forget about the tunnel. Perhaps Jim would decide to stay here overnight, and they wouldn't go through the tunnel until tomorrow. Or would that make it worse, Barney wondered – with more time to work himself into a state of shivering panic?

Jim moored up, and he and Barney went into the canalside store for some shopping. Into Jim's basket went baked beans, a loaf of bread, a litre of milk, a packet of dog treats and two tins of meat for Barney.

"Now for the tunnel," Jim said, knowing
that Barney didn't like it. "We'll soon be on
the other side."

Tail and ears low, Barney jumped
aboard. Jim put the food away in the galley,
then went to the rear of the boat to start
the engine.

Waiting at the stern, ready to dart indoors as soon as the tunnel mouth loomed, Barney looked back wistfully at the crowded canalside, wishing they could stay a bit longer.

Then he noticed that Jim had dropped
something outside the shop door. The dog
treats! It would be a pity to leave the
packet there, especially as Barney usually
had some as a reward for going through
the tunnel. Barney
gave a quick *whuff*
so that Jim would
see what he was
doing, then
bounded ashore,
ran back to the dropped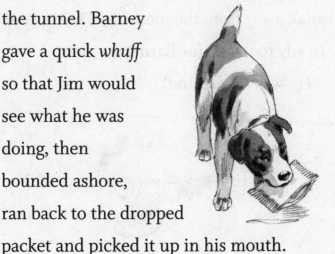
packet and picked it up in his mouth.

The wrapper was shiny and slithery and
he dropped it the first time. He bent down
for a better grip, picked up the packet and
turned to run back, expecting Jim to be
waiting, pleased that he'd noticed.

Jim wasn't looking.

Jim hadn't heard Barney's *whuff* above the roar of the engine starting up. He'd put on his raincoat, ready for the tunnel, and he was steering *Whistling Jack* out into the canal, away from the mooring. The gap was already too wide for Barney to jump.

He was left behind!

Chapter Three

Barney dropped the packet of treats and barked as loudly as he could. But Jim was steering away, waving to someone in a boat coming the other way and not looking back. He must have thought Barney was on his bunk, curled up on his blanket, ready for the tunnel.

Barney could easily run as fast as
Whistling Jack could go – faster, when he
was feeling really energetic. He left the
packet where it was and started to run. But
he'd hardly started when he collided with a
fence of legs – a group of people walking
towards him. One of them bent down and
grabbed his collar.

"Wait a minute, dog! You've dropped
something! You don't want to lose
this."

Barney didn't care about the dog treats
any more. The hand on his collar was kind
but firm, leading him back the wrong way,
towards the shop. Barney picked up the
packet and scampered off as fast as he
could after *Whistling Jack*. But, as he
rounded the bend, *Whistling Jack* was

already being swallowed by the circle of blackness. And there was no towpath through the tunnel.

Barney stood at the entrance and barked as loudly as he could. That other dog was in there, barking back. The dog with the fierce echoey voice was telling him to keep out.

"What's the problem, dog? Missed your boat?"

Barney turned round. Another narrowboat, *Tigerlily*, was coming slowly towards him, and a friendly-looking woman was standing on the foredeck, holding a mug of tea.

"Want a lift?" she called to him, and then she turned round and shouted to the man at the back who was steering. "Bill! Pull over a minute! There's a dog here that needs a ride through the tunnel!"

As the boat pulled over to the bank, Barney jumped aboard, dropping the packet at the woman's feet.

"Paying your fare, are you?" She laughed and bent to pick it up. "Thanks! Okay, Bill, ready!"

Barney crouched on the floor. The front doors of *Tigerlily* were closed, so he couldn't dart in and find a comforting bed to hide on while they went through the tunnel. He'd have to be brave. They'd soon be at the other end, and Jim would have stopped as soon as he realized what had happened. Even if he hadn't, they'd catch up at the next lock gate. They weren't far behind.

Tigerlily's headlamp cut through the darkness. Barney closed his eyes and

thought about rabbits in sunny meadows.
Cold water from the roof dripped on his
back and ears, and he tried not to
think of that fierce angry dog who lived
in the dark.

"Nearly there, dog." The *Tigerlily* woman
didn't sound at all afraid – like Jim, she
didn't understand what a dangerous place

the tunnel was. Barney opened his eyes as the last bit of dripping roof slid over his head. The glare of sunlight dazzled him. *Tigerlily* rounded a bend in the canal, and as his eyes cleared Barney saw, moored to the bank a little further on, *Whistling Jack*. Never had it been a more welcome sight, with its gleaming paintwork and its roof garden.

Barney barked with joy, expecting Jim to be there, waving and delighted.

"That's your boat, is it? PULL OVER, BILL!" the woman shouted. "Off you go, then." She gave Barney a farewell pat on the head. "Don't get left behind again!"

As soon as *Tigerlily* drew near enough, Barney jumped across to the foredeck of *Whistling Jack*. It was all quiet. The doors were closed and the padlock locked.

Jim was nowhere to be seen.

Barney's tail drooped with
disappointment. Where could Jim
have gone?

He jumped up and ran all the way along
the roof, to check the rear deck. No sign of
Jim. The doors at both ends were locked.

He ran back towards the tunnel, unsure what to do next. Then he realized what must have happened. Where the black mouth of the tunnel opened, a gentle green hill rose above, with a footpath leading up to a level ridge. This was another way of getting from here to Hayford Lock – you could walk over the top. Jim must have realized Barney was missing, and had walked back to find him.

On board *Tigerlily*, Barney had thought his problem was solved. But now he had a new one. He and Jim were at opposite ends of the tunnel!

Chapter Four

Jim had steered *Whistling Jack* all the way through the tunnel, out into the sunshine and round another bend before he realized Barney was missing.

He whistled loudly and waited for Barney to appear from his bed in the cabin, bouncing with delight as he always did.

Nothing.

"Barney? Aren't you coming up?" he called.

Still nothing. Jim pulled over to the side, then went down into the cabin and saw Barney's blanket, smooth and untouched since the morning.

He searched the whole length of *Whistling Jack*. No Barney.

Jim tried not to panic. Barney would never run away, he knew that. Not even to avoid going through a tunnel. Jim tried to remember exactly the last time he'd seen him. They'd been together in the shop, he knew that, because someone had patted Barney and said, "What a lovely little dog! Such a clever face." And then they'd gone out, and he'd seen Barney jump aboard –

he was sure of that. Almost.

Well, Barney certainly wasn't here now. There was only one thing for it – go back and find him.

It was difficult to turn the boat round in this narrow stretch of canal. The easiest thing would be to moor up, lock the doors and walk back over the top.

Jim started off at a run, up the slope and along the top, above the tunnel. He wasn't awfully fit for running, and a painful stitch in his side soon made him slow to a jog-trot.

Hayford Lock came into sight as he slithered down the steep bit at the other end. His eyes scanned the busy canalside. There were several narrowboats moored up, people wandering about, aiming cameras and looking into the tunnel, and several dogs sniffing around – but no Barney.

Where *was* he?

Almost in despair, Jim went from boat to boat, asking everyone if they'd seen a small brown and white dog.

"Yes – nice little dog with brown floppy ears? Saw him getting on a boat," said a man who was filling up the water tank of a boat called *Marigold*. "About twenty minutes ago. Went on through the tunnel."

Jim felt weak. He couldn't bear the thought of losing Barney. Had Barney been kidnapped? Lots of people liked the look of him. Had someone thought he was lost, and tried to help? But Barney had his name tag on – surely no one would keep him?

Jim tried to comfort himself. Barney was a clever dog – if he'd been kidnapped, he'd jump ashore as soon as he could. Jim thought he'd better go back to *Whistling Jack*; Barney would probably be waiting there. He tried to cheer up.

"Want a lift?" the helpful *Marigold* man said. "I'm about to set off. Come on board, if you like."

"Thanks," said Jim, and did.

Chapter Five

Barney decided that the best thing to do would be to wait. Jim would have to come back, sooner or later. He went as close as he could to the tunnel and waited in the shade of another boat that was moored there. He lay, nose on paws, looking towards the footpath, waiting for Jim to come into view.

Up on the slope, a family had been having a picnic. While Barney waited, they collected their plates and bottles and cartons and put them into a big basket, and walked down towards their boat.

"There's that dog again!" the boy said. "I saw him at Hayford Lock."

"What's he doing by our boat?" said the girl.

The father walked up to Barney. "Good boy! Let's have a look at your collar." He looked at Barney's collar disc and read, "*Whistling Jack*. Oh, I remember. *Whistling Jack* was moored up by the shop. I noticed it when we came through. Thought what an odd name it was."

"We might as well take him back with

us, if he's lost," said the mother.

No! Barney looked round and whimpered, trying to show them that *Whistling Jack* was just a little way round the next bend, not back at Hayford Lock at all. But they didn't understand.

"Don't worry. We'll soon have you back

on your own boat," said the boy. He lifted
Barney in his arms and carried him aboard
the boat, *Moorhen*.

"Put him down in the cabin, Kevin,"
shouted the father. "We don't want him
running off before we get there."

And Barney found himself shut in
a room with bunks, like the one on

Whistling Jack but twice as long and with four bunks instead of two. The door was firmly closed.

He barked his protest, but the engine was already starting up, and moments later *Moorhen* was heading into the tunnel. When Barney jumped up to the porthole window to look out, he saw only black slimy walls. He gave a mournful whine.

He hated being shut in. And, even worse, he was going through the tunnel again – without Jim, and his tasty reward at the end.

At last, at last, the darkness outside changed to sunlight, and the door was flung open.

"Okay, dog. Here we are. Time for you to get out," said Kevin. He picked up

Barney, who squirmed, wanting to jump down.

"That's odd," the father was saying. "Can't see that boat now! It must have moved on. Funny we didn't see it coming through the tunnel. I only saw that one other boat. Can't remember its name."

"I can. It was *Marigold*," said the mother.

"Now what?" asked Kevin. "What shall we do with him now?"

"Perhaps we'd better hand him in at the shop. They'll hang on to him till someone comes to collect him," said the mother.

No! Barney was going to find Jim by himself. He gave a furious wriggle, surprising Kevin, who dropped him. With one bound, Barney jumped from *Moorhen's* deck to the shore, and rushed off along the towpath. He thought Kevin might run after him, but he looked back, saw the boy shrug, and knew he was safe. He'd escaped – now all he had to do was find Jim.

He expected Jim to be somewhere on the towpath, by the shop or the water-pump or the café. There were lots of

people about and Barney ran
from group to group,
whuffling hopefully. But
none of them was Jim.

"There he
is again!"
Someone was
pointing. "That
man was just asking about his dog – isn't
that the one?"

Barney ran past quickly, in case anyone
made a grab for his collar. He told himself
that there was no point in panicking. He
knew what must have happened this time.
Jim had come here, failed to find him, and
walked back over the top. All Barney had
to do was go back to *Whistling Jack*. He hid
behind a café sign until *Moorhen* left its

mooring and chugged off down the canal, and then he doubled back and ran up the steep slope over the hill.

Jim would be worrying about him! He ran as fast as he could, though he was beginning to feel tired with all this to-ing and fro-ing.

Only a few more minutes, and they'd be together again.

Chapter Six

"There's my boat," Jim said to the *Marigold* man at the other end of the tunnel. "If you pull over I'll climb across. Thanks for the lift."

"No trouble," said the *Marigold* man. "Hope you find your dog."

Jim hoped so too! Carefully, he climbed

over from deck to deck. He expected to see Barney waiting, paws propped up on *Whistling Jack*'s gunwale, but there was no sign.

He whistled. He called. He searched.

No Barney.

Oh, no! *Now* what?

Marigold had pulled away, the friendly man waving, and the only person in sight was a fisherman sitting on the bank, between *Whistling Jack* and the tunnel.

"What's up, mate?" asked the fisherman, when Jim had walked past him five times.

"I've lost my dog," Jim explained. "Small brown and white dog, a bit plump, with floppy ears and a cheeky face."

"Oh, *that* dog," the fisherman said. "Gone back through the tunnel, on a boat called *Moorhen*. The family who found him thought he was lost."

"Thanks," said Jim, wondering what to do now.

Perhaps the easiest thing to do would be to take *Whistling Jack* back to Hayford Lock. If Barney was there, then all three of them would be together again: Jim, the boat, and Barney.

He got on board, unlocked the doors, started the engine and steered along the

canal until he came to the winding hole.
It was the only place wide enough to turn
round. To do this, he had to steer the nose
into the winding hole's half-circle, bring
the back end round, and set off back the
way he'd come.

Then he put on his waterproof coat and steered back through the tunnel. Drip, drip, drip, came the cold water from the roof. The boat felt very empty, because Jim knew that Barney wasn't there in his usual place on the bunk.

Whistling Jack wasn't the same without Barney on board. It was just a boat, not a home. Jim remembered what it had been like in the house, after Annie died – the rooms full of her remembered voice, the garden full of plants she'd grown from seed. He *couldn't* lose Barney as well as Annie…

Jim whistled hopefully when he reached the end of the tunnel, expecting Barney to come bounding up the steps.

Eagerly he scanned the towpath at Hayford Lock. Surely he'd find Barney this time!

Chapter Seven

Barney was hot and tired by the time he'd run all the way over the top of the hill. Panting, he padded down the last slope and scanned the canal bank eagerly. Then his heart sank. No *Whistling Jack*. There was only a mooring post where *Whistling Jack* had been.

Barney stared, blinked, and stared
again. What had gone wrong this time?

He was so disappointed that he flopped
to the ground. He felt dizzy with
muddlement. *Now*

what was he
going to do?
Had Jim got
fed up with
waiting and
carried on?

No, of course not. Jim wouldn't do that.
There was only one person in sight – a
fisherman, who stared at Barney with his
mouth open.

"Well, blow me down! That dog again!"
He was sitting on a low stool with his
lunch and his bait spread out beside him,

but now he got up and came towards
Barney. Barney watched him suspiciously.
He'd already been caught twice today and
he didn't want to be caught again.

"Come on! There's a good boy!" the
fisherman coaxed, and held out a piece of
stale bread.

Barney wasn't hungry and he didn't like
the way the fisherman was stalking
towards him. He lay still, his eyes keen.
Suddenly, the fisherman's hand darted out
and grabbed at his collar. Barney bounded
away, but the fisherman was more agile
than he looked. Already tired, Barney
didn't have much energy for a chase and
the fisherman was close behind, his long
arm reaching out. There was only one thing
to do. Barney gave a yelp, launched himself

into the air and plunged into the canal.

Wuuuuurghhhh!

The cold waters closed over his head
and filled his mouth and his eyes and his
nose.

Scrabbling, he rose to the surface, shook
the water out of his ears and looked back
towards the bank.

The fisherman was there, waiting. "Oi! Come back! I'm only trying to help!" he shouted.

Barney didn't dare to believe him. All he knew was that if he swam back to the bank, he'd be caught and taken somewhere he didn't want to go. He carried on swimming, doggy-paddle, looking back over one shoulder. And before he knew it he was swimming into the mouth of the tunnel.

He tried not to panic. At least the fisherman couldn't catch him in there. If he kept swimming, he'd eventually be back at Hayford Lock.

He didn't like it in the tunnel. He didn't like it even when he was safely on board *Whistling Jack*, and it was far worse now!

The roof arched above him, dripping. The engine smoke that gathered in the tunnel got into his mouth and nose, choking him as he gasped for breath. The water around him was black and cold. And worst of all, there was that other dog in here, the one that barked and told him to keep out. He couldn't hear a barking dog at the moment – only the splashing water and the pounding of his heart. He was a good swimmer, but he'd already been tired when he started, and now the tunnel seemed longer and darker than ever. As he doggy-paddled farther in, the sunlight from the entrance faded, and he could barely see a semi-circle of light at the end. He was swimming more and more slowly. Perhaps he'd never get there! He'd have to give up

swimming and let himself sink, and then the fierce barking dog would be waiting for him under the water…

Fear made him swim faster, pressing his ears back so that water wouldn't splash into them. And then something behind him filled the tunnel with golden light, so that he could see every seam in the brickwork and every watery weed that clung there. He looked over his shoulder. A boat was coming, its headlamp blinding him. A dark figure stood on the foredeck, pointing.

Chapter Eight

Jim?

No, the figure was too small and thin for Jim.

Barney swallowed a mouthful of water in his disappointment, and paddled onward. The boat was gaining on him, and he heard a girl's voice call out, "Mum!

Mum! It's a *dog!* A dog swimming!"

The engine slackened, and the dark figure was joined by a taller one.

"Fetch the boathook, Daisy," a second voice said. "Quick!"

Barney didn't know whether he wanted to be rescued or not. While he was wondering, he felt the cold metal of a boathook slip underneath his collar, and next moment he was pulled towards the boat and lifted out of the water, dangling and dripping.

He could hardly breathe! He just had time to see the boat's name, *Anna Belinda,* before he was plonked down on the deck. Water streamed from him, making a big puddle. He shook himself.

"Poor little thing!" said Daisy, wiping

herself down. "He must have swum in by mistake."

"He looks half-drowned," the mother said. "Take him below and wrap him up in a towel."

"He's wearing a name-disc, look!" said Daisy. She lifted it and read, "Barney."

"Barney? I wonder if he belongs to that boat that's usually moored up by the third lock past the tunnel? You know the one – *Barneycoot*," the mother said. "We'll stop as we go past, and ask."

No! No! Read the other side of the disc! Barney tried to signal with his eyebrows, but Daisy only said, "Poor thing. He looks as if he's got a bad cold. I'll go and get him dry."

She took him down to the galley and wrapped him in a huge towel. Then she stood him on a bench seat and rubbed him energetically. Barney began to feel warmer and even a bit sleepy, but he knew he must *do* something – otherwise he'd be taken three locks down in the wrong direction and delivered to a boat called *Barneycoot*.

Daisy was kind, but he wished he could
make her understand. She fetched him a
bowl of bread and milk, but he took no
notice, even though he was beginning to
feel quite peckish. They were coming out
of the end of the tunnel, into dazzling
sunlight, and there, moored up by the
canalside, was *Whistling Jack!*

Barney barked frantically and struggled to free himself. Jim was there, sitting on the foredeck with his head in his hands. He was just a few metres away!

Wriggling wildly, Barney tried to paw at the window to attract attention, but he was all tangled up in the towel. Before he could get himself free, *Anna Belinda* had slid past, and Jim was out of sight. Barney gave a whimper of despair.

"Oh, you poor thing," Daisy said. "You really are hungry, aren't you?"

Barney stared at her and tried to shake his collar so that the disc would flip over and she could read the other side, but she only said, "What's the matter? Water in your ears? Never mind. We'll soon have you home. Then you can dry out properly in the sun."

"Daisy! Come and help with the lock gates!" the mother shouted.

"Stay there. I'll see you in a minute," Daisy told Barney, and went up the steps.

This was his chance! Barney knew about lock gates. Both Daisy and her mother would be busy for a few minutes, and he could jump ashore. He scrambled free of the towel, jumped to the floor and ran up to the front deck.

The lock gates were ahead, and Daisy was heaving the first one open. That meant that the water in the middle of the lock was already at the same level.

"The dog's got out," Daisy's mum called from the back of the boat. "You'd better shut him up till we get through the locks."

"In a minute," Daisy called back.

He'd have to be quick!

The lock gate was open, and *Anna Belinda* slid gently through into the space between the two gates. Now Daisy had to close the first gate, then wind the key to let the water through the second, so that the water level would go down. Barney heard the gush of water as the sluices opened, and immediately *Anna Belinda* started to sink down as the water level lowered. The brick sides of the lock were just in reach, but if he waited any longer they'd be too high above him. He jumped up to the roof, crouched, and sprang.

"The dog!" Daisy's mum shouted. "Catch him!"

The brickwork was slippery. Barney scrabbled and slid, hanging by his front paws. He mustn't let go! He kicked wildly with his back legs, heaved himself over the ledge and was up, panting.

"*Here*, dog! Don't run away!" Daisy shouted. She ran towards him. Barney trotted over the closed lock gate and bounded off along the other side of the canal, as *Anna Belinda* sank out of sight.

Chapter Nine

Jim hadn't felt so hopeless since Annie died. He sat on *Whistling Jack*'s roof, slumped and sad.

"I'll never find him now!" he thought. "He's been kidnapped, I'm sure of it!"

Loneliness wrapped him in a cloak of misery. He didn't know what to do – he couldn't sit here for ever. But he couldn't even *think* of going on his way without Barney.

Inside the shop, the shopkeeper had been watching Jim for the last half-hour. Someone had told her he'd lost his little dog, and she felt sorry for him.

"Poor chap!" she thought. "He needs cheering up. I'll take him out a nice ice-cream cornet."

She went to the freezer, and made up an extra-large triple cornet of pistachio, walnut fudge and raspberry ripple ice cream. Then she stuck a chocolate flake in the top and went out to the towpath and *Whistling Jack*.

Barney, galloping back from the lock, had almost run out of energy, but the sight

of *Whistling Jack* made him speed up. When he saw how mournful Jim looked, sitting there by himself, he managed one last burst, and launched himself at Jim. It was unfortunate that, just at that moment, the shopkeeper was reaching up to Jim with the extra-large triple ice-cream cornet and Jim was jumping down from the roof of the boat saying politely, "That's really kind of you, but I don't think I—"

Wham! Splat! Splurge!

Jim's mouth opened wide as a mixture of Barney, pistachio ice-cream, walnut fudge and raspberry ripple flew into his face. The chocolate flake soared into the air and landed on the towpath. Jim almost fell backwards into the canal, clutching Barney, who licked and wriggled in delight. He liked ice cream, especially raspberry ripple.

Twenty minutes later, when they were ready to set off through the tunnel, Barney noticed the chocolate flake melting on the towpath. He wasn't supposed to eat chocolate, but still it would be a pity to waste it. If he jumped down quickly…

No. Perhaps it had better stay there.

Chapter Ten

Soon after, still feeling rather dazed and amazed, Jim and Barney were ready to continue on their way.

"If only I could explain to him what happened!" Jim was thinking.

"If only I could explain to him what happened!" Barney was thinking.

Barney sat beside Jim on the aftdeck as *Whistling Jack* pulled away from the canalside. The woman from the shop waved, and Barney licked the last taste of raspberry ripple ice cream from his whiskers.

They would soon be at the tunnel, but Barney wasn't going down to his bed in the cabin. He didn't intend to leave Jim's side, not even for a minute.

Jim reached down from the tiller and patted Barney's coat. It was still damp.

"Well, I don't know what he's been up to, but he's certainly been in the canal," Jim thought, "and he's been through the tunnel at least twice. Even though he hates it. Perhaps he *swam* through the tunnel? I wonder?"

He steered towards the tunnel entrance. Barney shivered a little, but stayed where he was, pressed against Jim's legs.

Jim had an idea.

"I know what I'll do!" he told Barney. "Next time we get to town, I'm going to find an engraver. And I'm going to get some extra letters engraved on your name tag. *Barney*, it'll say, *V.B.D.* That stands for Very Brave Dog."

Barney wagged his tail, so that it thumped on the deck. "It's almost as if he understands," he thought.

"It's almost as if he understands," Jim thought.

Not many dogs have letters after their name! Barney sat proudly, staring at the black mouth of the tunnel, waiting for *Whistling Jack* to slide in, out of the sunlight. He didn't think he'd ever actually *like* this tunnel. But he'd never be quite so scared of it again, not now he'd swum in it, and been through it in three strange boats.

After all, he was a Very Brave Dog now. And that was official.

Look out for
Barney the Boat Dog's
new adventure:

ISBN 9781409521990

Barney and Jim have to deliver a special
birthday present when their boat breaks down.
Puzzle the horse steps in to help. But he
turns out to be quite a handful...

Cat Tales

Curl up with Cat Tales, also by award-winning storyteller Linda Newbery. Look out for:

The Cat with Two Names

Two of everything leads to double trouble for Cat...

ISBN 9780746096147

Rain Cat

Is the mysterious cat really controlling the weather?

ISBN 9780746097281

Smoke Cat

Where do the shadowy cats in next door's garden come from?

ISBN 9780746097298

Shop Cat

Strange things have been happening since Twister arrived...

ISBN 9780746097304

The Cat who Wasn't There

Who is the little white cat in Vincent's garden?

ISBN 9780746097328

Ice Cat

A cat made of snow and ice can't come to life...or can it?

ISBN 9780746097311

For more fun and furry
animal stories visit

www.fiction.usborne.com